E
BOU

DATE DUE

PRINTED IN U.S.A.

From an episode of the animated TV series *Franklin and Friends*, produced by Nelvana Limited/Infinite Frameworks Pte. Ltd.
Based on the Franklin books by Paulette Bourgeois and Brenda Clark.

TV tie-in adaptation written by Harry Endrulat.
Based on the TV episode *Franklin's Christmas Spirit*, written by John van Bruggen.

Kids Can Press acknowledges the financial support of the Ontario Arts Council, the Canada Council for the Arts and the Government of Canada, through the CBF, for our publishing activity.

Published in Canada by
Kids Can Press Ltd.
25 Dockside Drive
Toronto, ON M5A 0B5

Published in the U.S. by
Kids Can Press Ltd.
2250 Military Road
Tonawanda, NY 14150

www.kidscanpress.com

Edited by Yasemin Uçar
Designed by Muse Communications

This book is limp sewn with a drawn-on cover.
Manufactured in Buji, Shenzhen, China, in 3/2013 by WKT Company

CM PA 13 0 9 8 7 6 5 4 3 2 1

Library and Archives Canada Cataloguing in Publication

Endrulat, Harry
       Franklin's Christmas spirit / Harry Endrulat.

(Franklin and friends)
Based on the character by Paulette Bourgeois and Brenda Clark.

ISBN 978-1-894786-90-4

1. Franklin (Fictitious character : Bourgeois) — Juvenile fiction. I. Bourgeois, Paulette II. Clark, Brenda III. Title. IV. Series: Franklin and friends

PS8609.N37F7396 2013   jC813'.6   C2012-908573-1

Kids Can Press is a *Corus* Entertainment company

Franklin's Christmas Spirit

Kids Can Press

FRANKLIN and his friends were very excited. Christmas was only a few days away! They were making special ornaments for their tree at school.

All the adults in Woodland were so busy buying presents, putting up their trees and decorating that they didn't seem to be having any fun at all!

"With Christmas, Hanukkah and Kwanzaa so near, this is a very special time of year," said Mr. Owl. "Sometimes things get so hectic, we forget what's really important and lose the holiday spirit."

"Now, we have an important decision to make," said Mr. Owl. "Play outside for recess, or stay inside and start decorating our tree?"

Rabbit hopped up and down. "I want to go outside and play in the snow!"

"Can I stay in and decorate?" asked Snail.

"Of course you may — if everyone else agrees," said Mr. Owl.

"Fine with me. We can finish our fort," said Franklin.

The rest of the class agreed.

Franklin and his friends bundled up and
went outside. Snail got ready to decorate the
tree. He looked up … and up … and up.

"That tree sure is high," said Snail. "Maybe
I should have asked for help."

But it was too late. There was no one else
around.

"I can do this," said Snail.

He took a deep breath and started to climb.

Snail hung a Santa ornament, then a purple ball, then a candy cane, then the garland.

When everyone came in from recess, the tree was almost finished!

"The tree looks great!" said Goose.
"Wow! You did this all by yourself, Snail?" asked Franklin.
"Once I got going, I couldn't stop," laughed Snail.
Franklin grabbed his ornament. "I can't wait to put up mine!" he said.

The rest of the class joined in to help trim the tree. When they were finished, they stood back to admire their work.

"Too bad there isn't more holiday spirit like this in Woodland," said Goose.

This gave Franklin an idea.

"Hey! What if we go *caroling*?" said Franklin. "I bet that would get everyone into the Christmas spirit!"

"That's a great idea," said Snail. "We'll need some fun songs — ones that I can play on my harmonica."

"Let's ask Aunt T," suggested Franklin. "She knows lots of great tunes."

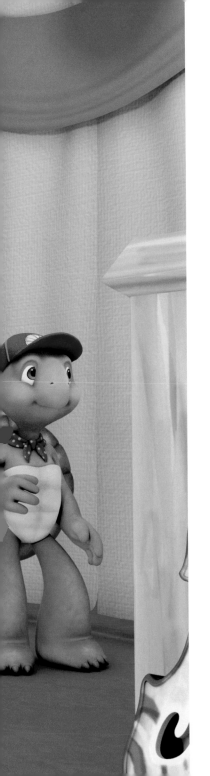

After school, Franklin and his friends called on Aunt T.

"A very merry Christmas to you all!" said Aunt T. "How can I help you?"

"We need a song to boost everyone's holiday spirits," said Franklin.

"I have just the thing," said Aunt T. She sat down at her piano. "It's called 'Christmas Cheer' and it goes like this.

It's that time of year —
the holidays are here.
There's much to do,
but don't forget:
Make time for Christmas cheer!
With a ho-ho-ho
and a fa-la-la-la-la!
It's time for Christmas cheer!"

Franklin and his friends loved the song. They practiced it over and over until they knew it perfectly.

"Remember, we'll meet tomorrow in the town square at four o'clock," said Franklin, as everyone prepared to leave.

"Will you come hear us sing?" Beaver asked Aunt T.

"I wouldn't miss it," said Aunt T.

The next day, Franklin got ready to go caroling. He put on his boots, scarf, hat and mitts.

"Aren't you forgetting something?" asked his father.

"What?" asked Franklin.

"This sleigh bell," said Franklin's father. "You can shake it as you sing."

Just then, Bear called. He had to help with his little sister and couldn't go caroling. Franklin hung up the phone and told his parents the news.

"That's too bad," said Franklin's father. "But it's nice of Bear to help his family. Now you'd better get 'dashing through the snow' or you'll be late."

Franklin sighed and headed for the town square.

He found Beaver waiting for him in front of the giant Christmas tree.

"Where is everyone?" he asked.

"They're all too busy helping their families get ready for Christmas. And I was just waiting here so I could tell you that I can't sing either. I have to help my mom deliver cookies. Sorry, Franklin," said Beaver, rushing away.

Franklin stood alone in front of the tree. He had lost his Christmas spirit.

Then he saw Snail.

"Hey, where is everybody?" asked Snail.

"No one else can make it," said Franklin. "So there won't be any singing today. I don't think I can do it by myself."

"That's how I felt when I wanted to decorate the tree at school," said Snail. "But I really wanted to, so I just did it!"

Franklin smiled. "You're right, Snail. I was excited to sing today, and that's what I'm going to do!"

Franklin jingled his sleigh bell and started to sing very quietly. He felt
nervous caroling by himself — until Snail joined in with his harmonica.
"Hey! We sound good together, Snail!" said Franklin.
"We sure do," said Snail. "Let's keep going!"
Franklin and Snail started the song again — only much louder this time!